Warriors of the Plains Tribes

Chris McNab

Cavendish Square
New York

This edition published in 2018 by Cavendish Square Publishing, LLC
243 5th Avenue, Suite 136, New York, NY 10016

First Edition

Website: cavendishsq.com

Cataloging-in-Publication Data

Names: McNab, Chris.
Title: Warriors of the plains tribes / Chris McNab.
Description: New York : Cavendish Square, 2018. | Series: Native American warfare | Includes bibliographical references and index. | Audience: Grades 6–10.
Identifiers: ISBN 9781502632869 (library bound) | ISBN 9781502633149 (ebook)
Subjects: LCSH: Indians of North America—Wars—Great Plains—Juvenile literature. |
Indians of North America—Great Plains—Juvenile literature.
Classification: LCC E78.G73 M259 2018 | DDC 978'.00497—dc23

Editorial Director: David McNamara
Associate Art Director: Amy Greenan
Production Coordinator: Karol Szymczuk

The photographs in this book are used by permission and through the courtesy of: All maps and black-and-white line artworks produced by JB Illustrations © Amber Books; AKG Images: 47 & 75 (North Wind Picture Archives), 162 (North Wind Picture Archives); Alamy: 98tr (North Wind Picture Archives); Art Archive: 128/129 (William E. Weiss/Buffalo Bill Historical Center), 194 (Buffalo Bill Historical Center); Bridgeman Art Library: 88/89 (Peter Newark American Pictures), 104/105bl (Peter Newark American Pictures), 120 (Look & Learn), 133 (Peter Newark American Pictures), 135 & 151 (Look & Learn), 174 & 197 (Peter Newark American Pictures); Corbis: 19 & 20 (Bettmann), 22t (Werner Forman Archive), 32 (Robert Wagenhoffer), 39 (Marilyn Angel Wynn/Nativestock Pictures), 42, 55 (Medford Historical Society Collection), 56/57 (Historical Picture Archive), 58 (Historical Picture Archive), 62 (Nik Wheeler), 63, 64, 83 (Bettmann), 86 (Peter Harholdt), 112, 137, 143, 146, 152, 157, 158, 159, 160 (Bettmann), 161 (Poodles Rock), 165tr, 165b (Tria Giovan), 176, 184 (Bettmann), 192 (Werner Forman Archive), 206, 209, 210, 211, 214/215 (Bettmann) Dorling Kindersley: 105t (Geoff Brightling) Getty Images: 8 (Bridgeman Art Library), 11 (Roger Viollet), 15 (Joe Sohm/Visions of America), 25 (Time & Life Pictures), 29 (Marilyn Angel Wynn/Nativestock Pictures), 36, 48 & 74 (Bridgeman Art Library), 78br (Science & Society Picture Library), 79tr & 97 (Hulton Archive), 140 & 145 (Time & Life Pictures), 148 (SuperStock), 150 (Bridgeman Art Library), 170/171 (Hulton Archive), 177 (Hulton Archive), 178 (Marilyn Angel Wynn/Nativestock Pictures), 193 (Bridgeman Art Library), 204/205, 207 (Hulton Archive); iStockphoto: 153 (Duncan Walker); Library of Congress: 9, 12/13, 17, 27tr, 41, 45, 49, 50/51, 54, 59, 65tl, 65b, 70, 72tr, 76, 85tl, 85br, 98bl, 100, 106, 109tl, 111, 115, 117, 118, 119, 121, 125, 127tr, 130, 139, 141 (both), 144, 154/155, 156, 163, 164, 167, 168 & 169 (all), 180 (both), 183 & 183 (both), 185, 187, 188, 195, 198/199, 200, 208; Mary Evans Picture Library: 81, 147, 181; Photos.com: 78/79tl, 90, 91, 109b, 127b, 172, 175; Photoshot: 6/7 (World Illustrated), 22bl & 113 (UPPA), 179 (UPPA); Public Domain: 72bl, 122; TopFoto: 102/103 (Granger Collection), 138 & 191 (Granger Collection); U.S. Department of Defense: 213; Werner Forman Archive: 27b (Ohio State Museum), 202 (Anthropological Museum of Lomonosov, Moscow).

Printed in the United States of America

CONTENTS

INTRODUCTION

Plains Indians is a blanket term for the tribes that extended from Alberta in Canada down to Texas in the southern United States, and from the Mississippi to the Rocky Mountains. As the term "Plains Indians" suggests, these tribes lived and died in a territory characterized by sweeping plains and prairies—what came to be called the "big country." The nature of this terrain, as we shall see, governed Plains warfare, particularly in relationship to the acquisition of the horse from the seventeenth century onwards.

One of the major Plains tribes, the Blackfoot are part of the great tribes of the wider cultural area. Those include the Nez Perce, Cheyenne, Sioux (a blanket term incorporating the Lakota, Dakota and Nakota), Assiniboine, Plains Cree, Arapaho, Kiowa and Comanche. Yet while the history of the Northern tribes became, in part, intimately bound up with the history of Canada, south of the Canadian border (as it was established by the mid-1850s) the struggles and fate of the other Plains tribes was forged in the crucible of the expanding US frontier.

◀ A particularly epic representation of Custer's last stand, the American ranks being hacked down by attacking Plains Indians. Although highly dramatized, the painting captures the speed and aggression with which mounted Indians could attack.

CHAPTER 1

Road to Alienation

Evidence of human presence on the western Plains dates back to 10,000 BCE, and from that time until the intrusion of the Europeans, the Plains Indians lived in a timeless and largely nomadic fashion, hunting buffalo, fishing and periodically fighting wars among themselves. During the sixteenth century, Spanish settlers

Nez Perce Warrior
A mounted Nez Perce warrior, dressed for cold weather. In combat, his horse would be decorated with bright paints and symbols to inspire the warrior spirit in the animal. The Nez Perce tribe originally inhabited Idaho, southeastern Washington State and northeastern Oregon, and were pure hunter-gatherers.

▲ **As the settlers pushed west, they became vulnerable to hit-and-run raids from the Plains Indians. Here some Indians put on an intimidatory show of force, while the settlers take cover behind their mounts.**

▲ **A Native American Plains warrior brings down a buffalo with a lance. Hunting buffalo required precise skills with the lance—the main target was through the shoulder, striking at the heart and other major organs.**

travelling up from Mexico and the South began to make contact with the southern Plains tribes, and, for reasons we shall explore, horses became available to them from the Pueblo Indians, who in turn had acquired them from the Spanish. By the mid-eighteenth century, many of the Plains tribes were partially on horseback, while some (such as the Comanche) were entirely mounted.

Horses changed the face of Plains Indian society and warfare, but deeper changes were to come from the expanding American frontier. In 1803, the Louisiana Purchase brought vast swathes of central North America under US control, transferred from France, which was eager to fund its wars in Europe. The purchase made the western expansion of the American people inexorable, as they pushed out from the eastern United States into what seemed a limitless range of land. This expansion drove them directly into the territories of the Plains Indians, who even by the mid-1800s were still in control of huge territorial areas. Yet whereas many of the Eastern Indian tribes had capitulated to the settlers' growth by this time, the Plains Indians were ready for a fight.

The Slaughter of the Buffalo

There were two principal threats to the Plains Indian culture from the settlers. First, the settlers were voracious hunters, and began the steady process of slaughtering the North American buffalo herds on which the Plains Indians depended for their existence. Buffalo hides were used for clothing and for making tipis; buffalo meat was a major part of their diet, and the leftover bones were used for tools; and buffalo dung served as cooking fuel. Of course, the Indians themselves slaughtered buffalo in huge numbers, to support a total population that stood at around 239,000 people in 1872. Between 1872 and 1874, it is estimated that the Plains Indians killed around 1.2 million buffalo. Yet during the same period the settlers killed nearly 3.2 million animals, often just for the hide and sometimes just for sport. In fact, railway companies often allowed passengers to shoot buffalo from the carriages as the trains passed through the plains.

Furthermore, the wanton destruction of the buffalo appears to have been part of US strategy to clear the Indians from desirable lands. In 1874, Congress heard the testimony of Secretary of the Interior, Columbus Delano, who explained that "The buffalo are disappearing rapidly, but not faster than I desire. I regard the destruction of such game as Indians subsist upon as facilitating the policy of the government, of destroying their hunting habits, coercing them on reservations, and compelling them to begin to adopt the habits of civilization." By the end of the century, the buffalo herds of North America were essentially gone, reduced from millions of creatures to just a few hundred, saved at the last minute by Presidential reprieve.

Reservations

While the slaughter of the buffalo was underway, another piece of social engineering was being enacted against the Plains Indians. The Indian Removal Act of 1830 legislated that Eastern Indians were to be removed from desirable territories east of the Mississippi and resettled in other lands west of the river, thereby freeing up

Nez Perce War 1877

The Nez Perce war was a brutal conflict resulting from settlers attempting to turn Nez Perce land over to cattle grazing. The Indians fought a long retreat to Montana, winning almost every battle along the way, before a final showdown at Bear Paw Mountain that forced their surrender.

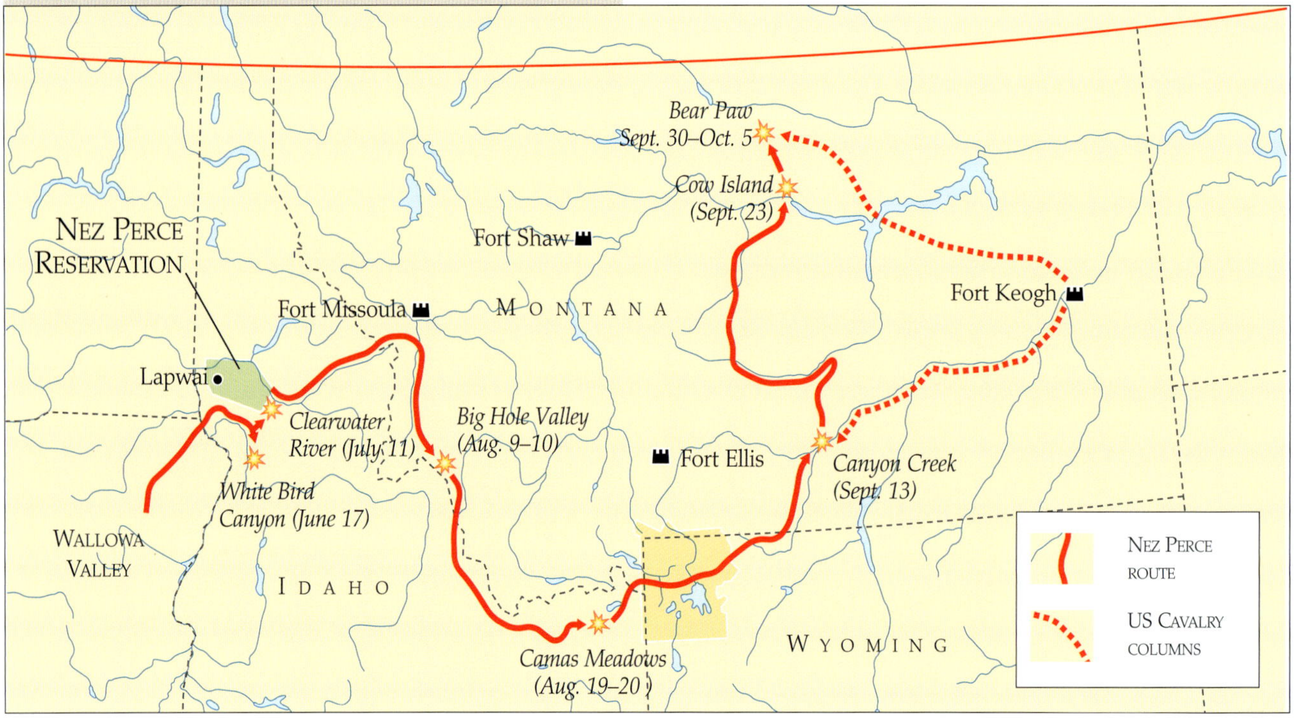

THE GRATTAN DEFEAT

In August 1854, a Lakota Indian killed a wandering cow in Wyoming. The Mormon owner of the cow, too afraid to go and look for it, reported that the Indians had stolen it, so 30 US soldiers under the command of Lieutenant John L. Grattan went to the Lakota village to forcibly reclaim the beast. The Indians were conciliatory at first, but they resisted Grattan's attempts to arrest their chief. In response, Grattan ordered his men to open fire, and the Indians retaliated—only one US soldier escaped alive. In consequence, the US government ordered a 600-strong force under General William S. Harney to take revenge, which they did by killing 85 Lakota and taking 70 women and children captive at the battle of Bluewater Creek in September 1885.

territories for the settlers. The act stipulated, among other clauses:

"Be it enacted by the Senate and House of Representatives of the United States of America, in Congress assembled, That it shall and may be lawful for the President of the United States to cause so much of any territory belonging to the United States, west of the river Mississippi, not included in any state or organized territory, and to which the Indian title has been extinguished, as he may judge necessary, to be divided into a suitable number of districts, for the reception of such tribes or nations of Indians as may choose to exchange the lands where they now reside, and remove there; and to cause each of said districts to be so described by natural or artificial marks, as to be easily distinguished from every other."

The language was legalistic and ordered, but the human fallout was traumatic and disastrous. The act resulted in conflict and expulsion, and drove Eastern tribes westwards towards the lands of the Plains Indians. By the mid-1850s, the Plains Indian themselves were targets of manipulative legislation, aiming to force them into reservations and allow settlers to utilize their land without recourse. The result was half a century of sporadic

SIOUX WAR 1862

The Sioux War of 1862 consisted of a series of battles in Minnesota as the Plains Sioux attempted to expel the settlers from their territory. Up to 800 settlers were killed by the Indians, one of the highest civilian death tolls in US history, but they were eventually overwhelmed by US forces.

Sioux Chief in Headdress
A Sioux chief is here seen in a full eagle feather war bonnet. The war bonnets were not just items of impressive decoration, but the arrangements and types of feathers used carried varying spiritual and military significance from tribe to tribe. In Sioux culture, an eagle feather war bonnet was one of the highest declarations of warrior skill, an item of clothing that carried obligations to future courage as well as a testimony to past bravery.

conflict, ranging from small-scale clashes to major wars. The Sioux Nation in particular fought regular wars with the US federal authorities from 1854 to 1890, the first war precipitated by a fabricated account that Lakota warriors had stolen a settler's cow (see "The Grattan Defeat," above).

Officially, the US government often appeared to be seeking reasonable solutions, but in practice it allowed every treaty to be violated by the settlers, then took revenge against Plains tribes who took up arms to resist the intrusions. The Indian Wars saw four decades of atrocity and counter-atrocity, as well as the Federal forces suffering some substantial losses and defeats. For example, 800 settlers and soldiers died in the Minnesota Uprising of 1862, led by the Dakota chief Little Crow, and the US defeat at the Little Bighorn in 1876 has gone down as one of the most dramatic US military failures of the nineteenth century, outside of the Civil War.

Yet the end of the story is known—the Plains Indians ended up decimated and dispersed, their old way of life gone forever. Yet the reasons why they were able to keep the swelling force of the US Army on its toes for so long is the story of the remainder of this resource.

CHAPTER 2

Hunting and Warfare in the Prehorse Age

As the horse revolutionized Plains Indian warfare so completely, it is worth considering how the Indians hunted and fought before this seminal change. Looking at the Plains Indians during the 1500s, however, show us the important continuities as well as the contrasts. As we shall see, the Plains Indians developed long-standing techniques of hunting on foot that translated into mounted warfare from the seventeenth century onwards, and which were still used during the desperate wars of the nineteenth century.

What largely unified all the Plains Indian tribes was a culture that revolved around the rhythms and processes of buffalo hunting, a practice that had effects beyond mere subsistence activity. Indeed, the seasonal patterns of the buffalo—which dispersed into smaller groups in the winter when forage became scarce—affected tribal composition in a similar way. During the autumn and winter months, the tribe would often divide itself into smaller groups of families, these working as less-demanding hunting groups when compared to the full tribe. The lifestyle was largely nomadic, hence the tipi provided the ideal accommodation for the Plains Indians. In fact, a properly made tipi was windproof, waterproof, big enough for a decent-sized family and could be erected and dismantled in minutes by just two people.

Stealth Tactics
Two Indian scouts use animal skins to aid their observation of a US Army camp. Similar tactics were used during buffalo hunting, as the skins broke up the lines of the familiar human silhouette. There are accounts of Indians moving to within a few yards of settler soldiers while wearing such disguises.

When we look at the way the buffalo were actually hunted, we start to feel our way into the Plains Indian style of warfare. Buffalo are large, fast and dangerous animals, with an aggressive desire to protect their young, so intelligent, cooperative tactics were the root of Plains Indian hunting. When hunting small groups of buffalo, the basic technique involved simply stalking the animal from downwind, using cover and concealment to approach within bowshot. Sometimes the warriors would drape themselves in a wolf skin or other animal hide and crawl on all fours towards the target herd, the skin helping to both mask their scent and conceal their human appearance.

Tracking and Observation

A primary reason why so many Indians were employed as scouts by the US forces was their superlative skills in tracking and observation. By studying marks on trees and on the ground that were almost invisible to the untrained eye, an Indian scout could derive details such as how many men and horses had passed, whether some were injured or carrying weight and their direction of travel. They also had formidable powers of observation, as was attested by Edwin Denig, a fur trader in the 1850s who spent time with the Assiniboine:

"At a distance of 12 or 15 miles [19–24km] they will distinguish animals from timber, even supposing they are not in motion. If moving they will discern between horses and buffalo, elk and horses, antelope and men, a bear and a bull, or a wolf and a deer, etc. But the greatest mystery is how they make out anything living to be fair at such a distance, on the instant, when they themselves are in motion or the animal at rest. This they do when it is surrounded by a hundred other objects as like to living creatures as it is. Once pointed out, the movements are watched and its character thus determined. Their powers in this respect are truly astonishing and must be acquired. They also judge very correctly of the relative distances of objects either by the eye or to each other. Smoke can be seen rising on the plains at a distance of 60 miles, and they will tell from that or a lesser distance within a few miles of the place where it rises."

– *Denig* (1930)

Such tactics were fine for small numbers of animals, but a massive herd required far more dramatic strategies. There were two essential methods of hunting large buffalo herds on foot. The "piskin" involved the hunters forming themselves into a long "V" shape, the tip of the V terminating in either an enclosure or a sheer drop or escarpment. The hunters would channel the buffalo herd between them, startling it into a stampede that was funnelled down the V towards the enclosure, where they would be trapped, or fall off the edge of the escarpment. The second method, known as the "surround," is fairly self-explanatory—the hunters would form themselves around the herd in a large circle, then tighten the circle around the prey, shooting into the mass of panicking creatures with arrows and lances. This strategy involved greater risk of death and injury at the horns of a fear-demented buffalo, but it was also a test of the hunter's bravery and stamina, and doubtless provided good fireside stories.

THE HORSE

More than anything, it was the acquisition of the horse that changed the nature of Plains Indian hunting and warfare. Horses gave unprecedented mobility and speed, access to more distant territories and opportunities to develop new styles of warfare. The Plains Indians acquired horses during the seventeenth and eighteenth centuries. First contact with horses came to the Pueblo Indians through their relationship with the Spanish (see box feature, overleaf), but steadily horse ownership spread through the southern

Plains, aided by the 1680 Pueblo revolt, which saw the transfer of thousands of Mexican horses to the Plains Indians. By the mid-1700s, horse ownership had spread as far north as the Blackfoot tribe.

The Native Americans were almost preternaturally gifted horsemen. John Irving, writing in the 1830s, here recounts the subjugation of a mustang at the hands of a Plains Indian:

"A young Indian first came forward, and led up a bright, jet-black mare; after him followed another, holding in his hand a long buffalo tug, or halter, which restrained the wild motions of a two years" old colt ... At one moment he dashed swiftly around at the full stretch of the long tug which secured him—then pausing, and shaking his long mane over his head, he fixed the gaze of his almost bursting eyes upon his captor. Then raising his head, and casting a long, lingering, and almost despairing gaze upon the hills of the prairie, which till then had been his home, he made a desperate leap forward, dragging to the ground the Indian who held the end of his halter. Others, however, rushed to his assistance, and held him in. The crowd then attempted to close round him, but he reared upon his hind legs, and kept them at bay with rapid and powerful blows of his fore feet. At length a young Indian who was standing near, threw off his robe and crept cautiously towards the animal from behind. With a sudden leap he bounded upon his back, and seized the tug, which was secured in his mouth. Before this, the efforts of the animal had been violent; but when he felt the burden upon his back—when he felt the curbing hand of his rider—he sent up a shrill and almost frantic scream—he bounded in the air like a wild cat—he reared, he plunged, but in vain. His rider was a master hand, and retained his seat as unmoved as if he had constituted part of the animal itself. He curbed him in—he lashed him with his heavy whip, until he crouched like a dog upon the prairie. His spirit was crushed; and the last spark

Buffalo Hunting "Surround" Technique
An overhead diagram of Plains Indians hunting buffalo by using the "surround" technique. Such tactics, made possible by the acquisition of horses, were also used in combat against settlers, who tended to cluster around wagons or habitations.

of freedom was extinguished. Shortly after, one of the hunters came up and tied a pack upon his back. He made no resistance, and they led him off with the rest, to finish his days in drudgery and toil."

– *Irving* (1835)

Such accounts of Indian horsemanship are far from uncommon. Realizing the potential of the horse, the Plains Indians instructed their youth in horsemanship from the earliest age. Richard Hook notes that in the Comanche "both boys and girls were capable riders by the age of seven" and that a virtual big-top repertoire of trick riding skills were standard talents, such as the ability to lean out from a galloping horse and snatch a person or other object from the floor. When hunting buffalo on horseback, the hunters, mounted on the swiftest "buffalo-runner" mounts, could now run down selected prey, shooting them from horseback with either a bow or a gun. The same could apply to warfare, the horse giving the Indians the ability to move at speed around their enemies, disorientating them and providing targets of opportunity.

▼ A Native American man hunting buffalo on horseback, 1853. The ability to shoot and reload the bow from horseback gave Native Americans a distinct combat advantage against settlers armed with flintlock firearms.

Mounted Warfare

Until the nineteenth century, the bow was the most common weapon of the mounted Plains Indian; its rate of fire was higher than that of early firearms, and

Pueblo Indians

The Pueblo Indians, an ancient Native American tribe inhabiting what is today New Mexico and Arizona, had lived for centuries in the Southern territories before making contact with the Spanish during the late sixteenth century. "Pueblo" comes from the Spanish word for "town," the Spanish applying the label on account of the structural similarity of Pueblo Indian settlements to Spanish towns. They struck up a precarious relationship with their new European neighbors, hiring out their labor for work on Spanish settlements or farms.

Spanish attempts to convert the Pueblo to Catholicism, however, helped precipitate the Pueblo Rebellion of 1680–92, led by the Indian chief with the rather ironic (given the cause of the rebellion) name of Popé. The rebellion at first brought success for the Pueblo. They ejected the Spanish from Santa Fe, killing 400 of them, and largely drove the Spanish from the territory. Although the Pueblo then successfully resisted Spanish attempts at counter-attack, the integrity of the resistance was steadily undermined by Popé, who alienated himself from his people by dictatorial behavior. The rebellion progressively collapsed from within and, by 1696, the Spanish had reclaimed the territory they had lost.

▲ An adobe Pueblo settlement. Adobe consists of sand, clay and water, plus an additional fibrous material, and was shaped into dried bricks.

◀ A Cheyenne Indian on horseback. The introduction of the horse into Plains Indian culture not only provided a new vehicle of warfare, but dramatically increased the scale of tribal hunting territories.

it was more convenient to load and shoot on a jolting horse than a muzzle-loading musket. Nevertheless, there are plenty of accounts of Indians who did master handling flintlock firearms from horseback. An article in the *Literary Gazette*, dated 1836, provides an account of the life of Blackbird (c.1750–1800), chief of the Omaha Indians, whose territory was traditionally in modern-day South Dakota, Nebraska and Kansas. Blackbird was a true warrior, and the article describes a perfect fusion of horse and gun:

"In attacking a Kanza village, he rode singly round it, loading and discharging his rifle at the inhabitants as he galloped past them. He kept up in war the same idea of mysterious and supernatural power. At one time, when pursuing a war party by their tracks across the prairies, he repeatedly discharged his rifle into the prints made by their feet and by the hoofs of their horses, assuring his followers that he would thereby cripple the fugitives, so that they would easily be overtaken. He, in fact, did overtake them, and destroyed them almost to a man; and his victory was considered miraculous by friend and foe."

Allowing for some mythologizing, it was undoubted that the equal enthusiasm of Indians for guns and horses would have produced many talented firearms-equipped mounted warriors. This talent reached its peak of perfection during the nineteenth century, when fixed cartridge revolvers and magazine-fed rifles made the process of reloading on horseback that much simpler, and dramatically increased rates of fire (see below for a more extended discussion of percussion weapons).

The acquisition of horses in many ways actually increased the likelihood of armed conflict for the Plains Indians. Horse raiding became a major cause of localized armed conflict. Furthermore, horses

Crow Indian Horse
A Crow Indian horse in full regalia, including bridle, reins (braided rawhide), saddle (wooden frame covered in rawhide) and stirrups. The pendant hanging over the center of the horse's forehead, made from cloth and beads, represents the Morning Star.

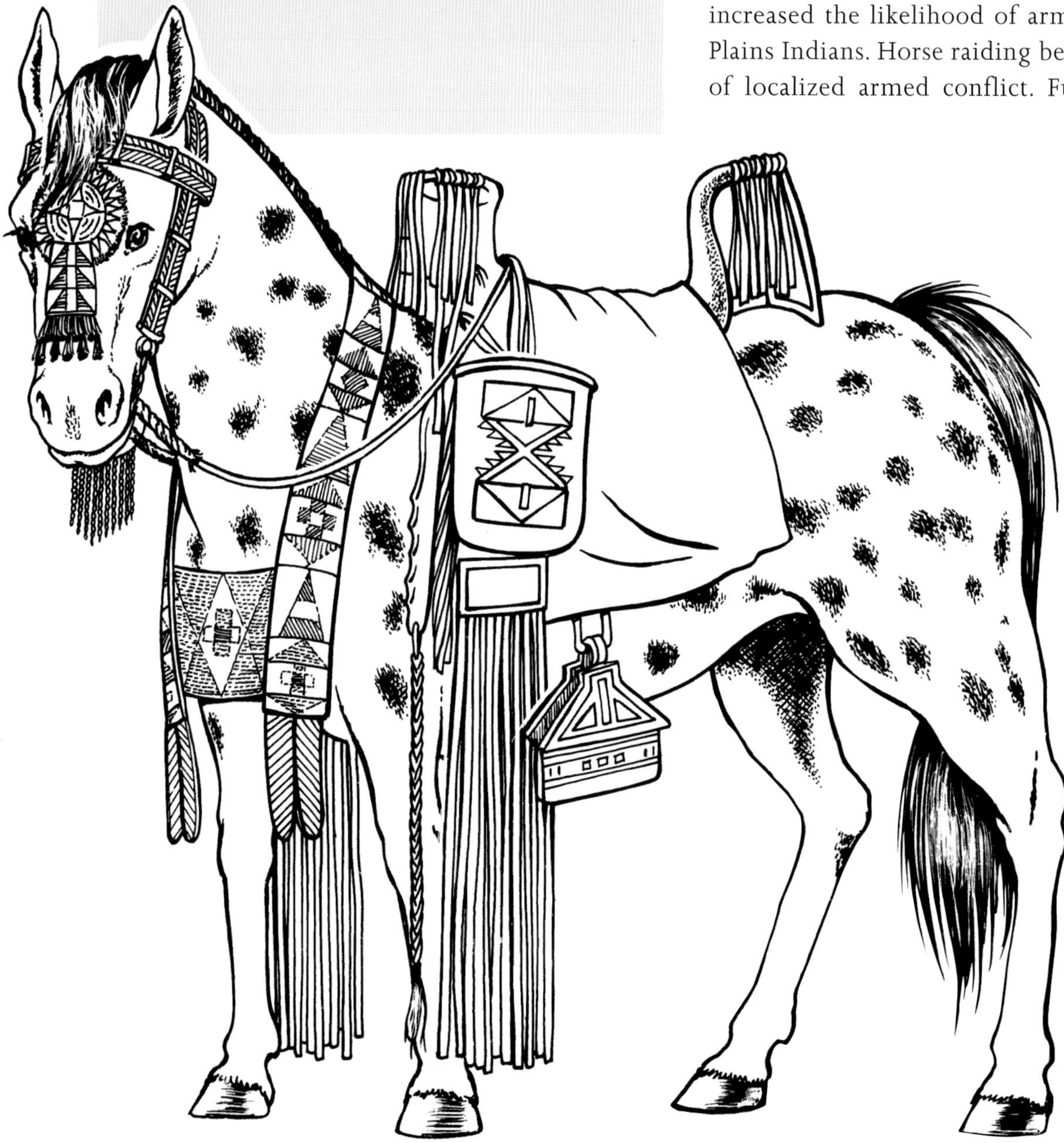

▲ A striking photograph of Crow Indians, all armed with long lances. The lance was originally a buffalo hunting tool, but was easily adapted to warfare.

enabled tribal warriors to venture further afield in search of buffalo and other food, and in so doing raised the possibility of coming into contact with similarly roaming hunters from other tribes. In fact, this possibility of previously unlikely contact with other tribes often became reality. A US government document from 1831, written by Indian agent Jos M. Street to the US Secretary of War, Lewis Cass, explains the friction between the Sioux Indians and the neighboring Sac and Fox. In one incident, the writer explains, three Sac Indians were out hunting when they spotted intruders in their territory:

"They [the Sacs] say they were only three in company, and perceived two Sioux in a prairie within the limits of the Sac and Fox lands hunting buffalo. One of the Sacs went towards the Sioux with professions of friendship, but the Sioux threw their blankets and breast cloths off, and shot him. The other two Sacs (who had been concealed from the Sioux), immediately pursued them, and killed both Sioux. They also say that they had no war party."

– *Street* (1831)

Such a local action was, as the writer implies in the document, just part of a general pattern of clashes emerging between the Sioux and the Sac and Fox tribes in the early 1830s. In balance to the episode just described, he goes on to explain a similar incident in which the Sac and Fox are the intruders:

"Four Sioux were hunting in a prairie, near the head of the Terre Bleu river, at a place called by the

Comanche Equipment
The Comanche had a broad range of traditional weapons to draw on, from rudimentary stone-headed clubs through to composite bows and firearms purchased from settler traders.

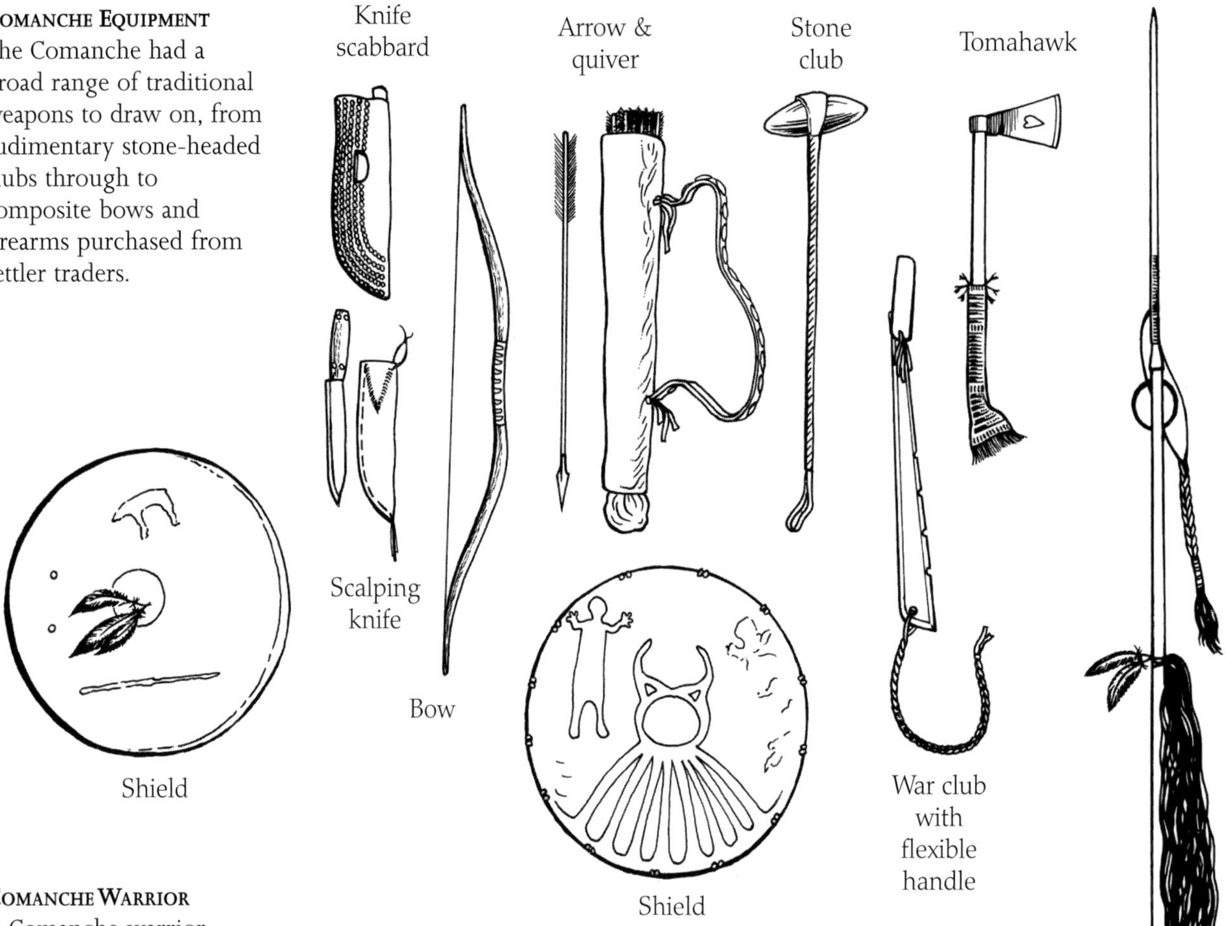

Comanche Warrior
A Comanche warrior prepares to deliver a lance strike while bringing his horse up the the gallop. The Comanche lances ranged in length from 8-14 feet (2.4-4.3m) long, with points of either knapped flint, fire-hardened wood or sharpened metal.

Indians "the Hill that stands up," about 70 or 80 miles [112–128km] north of the line of the land sold to the United States at Prairie des Chiens last year. They were surprised by ten Sacs or Foxes coming rapidly and unexpectedly upon them. The Sioux fled, and the Sacs fired and killed two of them. The remaining two Sioux turned, fired and killed one Sac or Fox, and effected their escape to the nearest encampment of Sioux."

– *Street* (1831)

A significant feature of this quotation is the reference to "land sold to the United States." Although such conflicts were intertribal, they were often intensified by the territorial dislocation caused by settler expansion and US land negotiations with the Native Americans. Street acknowledges this fact, and gives Cass a cautionary message regarding the Sioux state of mind:

"Major Taliaferro has no doubt fully apprised you of the state of feeling in which he left the Sioux, and the course it indicated, if left to themselves. To me, recently, they hold language like this: 'The treaty of 1830 [the Indian Removal Act of 1830] has been broken. Our land has been invaded and our people killed while quietly hunting meat for their families. We want satisfaction. Our fathers at Prairie des Chiens told us, if we were struck, not to revenge it; but to leave it to our great father the President, and he would see justice done us. We tell you now, that we will be quiet until the waters flow again in the spring. Then if our great father does not see justice done to us, we will wait no longer. We will revenge our brother warriors.'"

– *Street* (1831)

The explicit threat made by the Sioux was, as we have seen, ultimately realized in decades of bitter warfare between the Plains Indians and the US Army. For tribes whose very existence was based upon buffalo hunting, and whose use of horses gave them access to vast swathes of the land, any policy that ate into land ownership was bound to cause trouble.

CHAPTER 3

Weapons of the Plains Indians

Firearms

The Plains Indians were both beneficiaries and victims of firearms. This dual relationship with firepower was at no time more apparent than during the nineteenth century, when firearm design underwent several critical revolutions. In the second decade of the century came the invention of the percussion cap. This cap—a small brass cup filled with fulminate of mercury—rendered the flintlock system obsolete (although flintlocks remained in use for many years thereafter). Instead of a flint striking a steel above a pan of loose priming powder, the percussion cap system worked simply by placing the cap on a nipple under a hammer. When the trigger was pulled, the hammer dropped on the cap, detonating the fulminate of mercury through impact, and the resulting hot flame flashed down a vent in the nipple into the main chamber, igniting the main charge and firing the gun. Percussion weapons were more reliable and produced faster lock times (the time between pulling the trigger and the gun firing) than flintlocks.

Alongside a whole new generation of percussion long guns, the percussion system also led to the creation of true revolvers. By the 1830s, the firearms legend, Samuel Colt, was producing his first percussion-cap revolver, a five-shot handgun that, once loaded, could fire as quickly as the user could cock the hammer and pull the trigger. By the end of the Civil War in 1865, the United States was a land awash with handguns.

But even greater changes were to come. The percussion cap was superseded during the first half of the nineteenth century by the fixed cartridge, the system in which primer, powder and bullet were combined in a brass case. Space does not allow us to explore the full implications of the fixed metal cartridge, but its most important achievements were the dramatic acceleration of reloading times (particularly once allied to magazine feed), the perfection of breech-loading firearms (that ultimately offered more power than muzzle-loaders and made rifling a standard feature) and greatly improved reliability—there was no more loose powder to become damp or spilt.

By the time of the American Civil War, therefore, the world of firearms had been utterly transformed.

War Horses

Much like human warriors, Native American horses were also highly decorated to show their performance and status as warhorses, and to channel the spirits and powers on which the Indians relied. The painting was performed by the *Tsunkan-wakan* (Holy Horse) medicine man using red and white clay paint, and some of the classic symbols were as follows:

SYMBOL	MEANING
Antelope horns	Power, speed
Dragonfly	Protection
Representation of wounds	Illustrated places the horse had been wounded in battle
Outline of a man on horse's chest	Signified the horse had ridden down an enemy in battle
Zigzags down legs	Evoked the fear of the lightning spirit

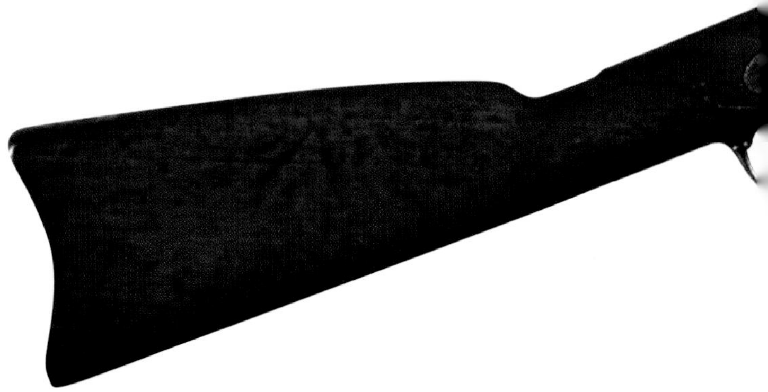

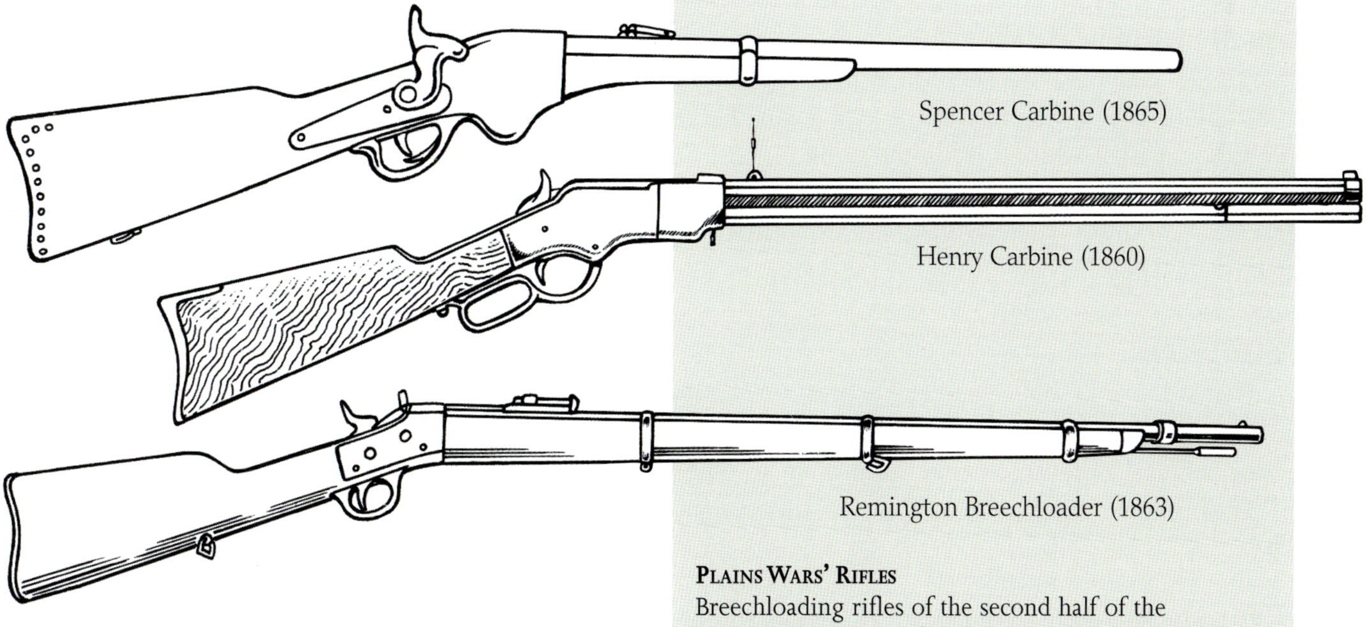

Plains Wars' Rifles
Breechloading rifles of the second half of the nineteenth century offered many qualities desirable to the Plains Indians. They had practical ranges of hundreds of meters, for example, and could be reloaded from horseback. The biggest problem was obtaining adequate supplies of ammunition.

For the Plains Indians, of most interest were the big "buffalo hunting guns," such as the powerful Sharps, Spencer, Springfield and Henry/Winchester rifles. The latter is a good example, albeit at the end of our period, to show how far firearms had come since the beginning of the century. Chambered in powerful big-game hunting calibers (such as .45-75 and .50-95 Express), the Winchester Model 1876, for example, could drop a buffalo or enemy accurately at several hundred meters and was fed from an 11-round underbarrel tubular magazine—all the operator had to do to reload was to cycle the lever attached to the trigger guard.

Yet Native Americans were essentially at the end of the firearms supply chain, acquiring often suspect quality firearms directly through trade, or taking weapons during raids and battles against the settlers. A problem that was never overcome, even in the age of fixed cartridges, was that of ammunition supply. The Plains Indians were excellent at maintaining and repairing their weapons, showing material ingenuity—broken stocks, for example, could be repaired with strips of rawhide.

They also treated their firearms as more than simple violent tools; many Indian rifles are decorated with brass studs along the woodwork, showing their status as aesthetic objects. Obtaining ammunition, however, was a constant problem, which probably accounts for the fact that although most Plains Indian warriors had acquired rifles by the 1870s, at the battle of the Little Bighorn in 1876 only around 30 or 40

▲ An 1873 Springfield trapdoor carbine. With its powerful .45-caliber round, the Springfield could kill buffalo and humans with ease. It was used both for and against the Plains Indians, and was wielded by figures such as the great Geronimo.

percent of the Native Americans involved in the battle actually used them in combat, the rest relying on their traditional weapons. Ammunition supply must have been complicated by the fact that one tribe would have multiple types of weapon. After the Little Bighorn, a study of cartridge cases at the site revealed that the Indians had used Henry, Winchester, Springfield, Remington and Sharps rifles, as opposed to the Springfield carbines and Colt revolvers issued to the Federal troops.

Plains Indians were generally slower to adopt handguns, at least as practical hunting and combat tools, because bows largely outclassed them in terms of performance. Yet handguns became increasingly common Indian side-arms following the American Civil War, when a glut of military-surplus weapons flooded the market. Illuminating our study of Plains Indians and firearms is a story from Charles S. Bryant, who in 1864 recounted the experience of Minnesota soldiers and settlers battling with hostile Sioux warriors. In one instance, Sioux warriors attacked a settler outpost, and two men began what seemed a very personal sniper duel:

"As an instance of the manner in which the fight was now conducted, we would mention a part of the personal adventures of Mr. Walter P. Hills, a citizen, who three times came as a messenger from the fort during the time it was in a state of siege. He had just returned to the post with dispatches from this office, the evening before the attack was made. He took part in the engagement, and killed his Indian in the early portion of the fight, before the enemy was driven across the river.

He afterward took position at one of the port-holes, where he paired off with a particular Sioux

▼ Plains Indians circle and attack a wagon train. For the settlers under such an attack, the best defense was to huddle together and put out withering fire from behind the wagons. A warrior party would typically break off the action once it had suffered a handful of casualties.

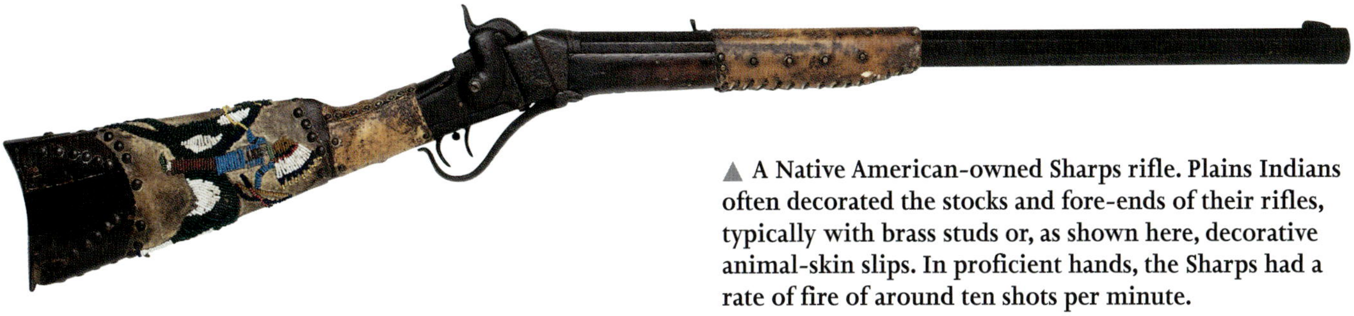

▲ **A Native American-owned Sharps rifle. Plains Indians often decorated the stocks and fore-ends of their rifles, typically with brass studs or, as shown here, decorative animal-skin slips. In proficient hands, the Sharps had a rate of fire of around ten shots per minute.**

warrior, posted behind a tree of his own selection. He, being acquainted with the language to a considerable extent, saluted and conversed with his antagonist, and as the opportunity was presented, each would fire at the other. This was kept up for about an hour, without damage to either party, when the Indian attempted to change his position, so as to open fire from the opposite side of his tree from that which he had been using hitherto. In this maneuver he made an unfortunate exposure of his person in the direction of the upper bastion of the fort. The report of a rifle from that point was heard, and the Indian was seen to make a sudden start backward, when a second and third shot followed in rapid succession, and Mr. Hills beheld his polite opponent stretched a corpse upon the ground."

– *Bryant* (1864)

The style of battle between these two men is reminiscent of stylized bow fights the two men speak with each other over the course of the hour-long shootout, occasionally letting off shots from behind cover. In classic Indian style, the Sioux warrior shoots from behind a tree, understanding that even the most powerful contemporary rifle would be unable to penetrate a substantial tree trunk. In fact, it is only his decision to change position, plus the exceptional marksmanship of his opponent, that results in his demise.

The Bow

However ingrained firearms became in Plains Indian society, the bow endured to the end of our period. Jim Hamm, an expert on the Native American bow, here explains the Plains Indian bow for mounted warriors:

"In the Plains area horsemen prevailed, and their bows were normally shorter than those used by Indian who hunted on foot (with the exception of the sinew-backed yew bows). The Plains bows were usually 50 inches [127cm], or shorter, and the handy, maneuverable weapons were ideally developed for horseback hunting or warfare. Rectangular in cross section, with the widest part of the bow being at the handle, most bows were 1 inch [2.5cm] to 1¼ inches [3cm] wide at the handle and about ¾ inch [1.9cm] wide at the tips. In pre-Columbian, pre-

▲ **A photographic portrait of a Crow chief in war paint. He carries a typical Plains Indian self-bow, of short dimensions and made from a single piece of wood.**

horse days the Plains bows were longer, and 55–60 inches [140–152cm], and comparable to bows used by historical foot Indians."

– *Hamm* (1989)

Hamm illustrates how the introduction of the horse changed the nature of bow construction. Prior to the horse, when most hunting and warfare was done on foot, bows were longer and more powerful, necessary for shooting at buffalo at long range. Once the Plains Indian warrior was mounted, however, bows had to be more compact, but any reduction in power was compensated by the ability to get closer to prey on horseback. In terms of the wood for the bows, chokecherry, wild plum, hickory, ash or crab apple were typical, backed with sinew. Arrowheads were, in earlier times, made from flint, but by the time of the Little Bighorn battle they were almost exclusively made from

Firing from Horseback

Firing a bow and arrow from horseback not only required experience to judge the right moment of release, it also needed perfect balance on the part of the rider. Mounted shots were typically taken at close to medium range, the rider allowing the horse to take him up to the target before drawing and firing in one swift movement.

iron, which was easier to fashion into shape and more durable while fighting.

The power of the Plains Indian bow was not to be doubted. A contemporary observation of the bow in action during a hunting expedition leaves no doubt as to its power as a weapon (see quotation, right). Such performance may relate to the longer, more powerful bows of the Plains Indians, but there is little doubt that whatever the design they would have been capable of serious and lethal penetration.

Other Weapons

Alongside the bow, the Plains Indians carried the typical assortment of clubs, trade knives, tomahawks and spears. They also carried shields and basic armor. Regarding the shields, the prehorse communities produced shields of several layers of buffalo hide, heat shrunk and hardened with glue made from buffalo hooves, sometimes padded with feathers, fur or other projectile-absorbing material. A typical shield would have measured around 3 feet 4 inches (1m) in diameter, but mounted warriors required something far more compact, these shields measuring 1 foot 8 inches-2 feet (0.5-0.6m) in diameter. Both historians and contemporaries have argued over the efficacy of such shields in relation to musket balls and rifle bullets. The percolated conclusion of the arguments is that the shields were capable of stopping a bullet from a low-velocity weapon, such as a handgun at long range, but against any powerful firearm they gave little protection. For the Indians who carried them, however, their efficacy was only partly bound up with their physical qualities. The "medicine" attached to the shield was equally if not more important. Like the war paint decorating warrior and horse, similar motifs were painted on shields, or they were hung with guardian elements such as feathers or animal claws. Great ritual and care was taken while preparing such shields. Richard Hook notes that:

"Shields were prevented from touching the ground, and kept on tripods facing the sun to renew their power. The belief in the shield's spiritual power was such that sometimes only the thin protective cover, a miniature of the shield or a lacework shield were actually carried into battle."

—*Hook* (1985)

"HE CARRIED A BOW AS LONG AS HE WAS TALL, WITH ARROWS OF PROPORTIONAL LENGTH, WITH WHICH HE COULD KILL GAME A HUNDRED YARDS [91M] DISTANCE. I KNEW AN INSTANCE OF THE TERRIBLE FORCE OF THESE ARROWS WHICH IS WORTHY OF NOTE. AIMED AT THE BEAR, THREE YEARS OLD, BUT HAD TAKEN REFUGE IN THE TOP OF A TREE, IT WENT THROUGH THE BRUTE'S BODY AND WAS PROPELLED FORTY OR FIFTY YARDS [37–46M] BEYOND."

– NEWCOMBE (1978)

Plains Indian armor was also produced from animal hides, often arranged in a double thickness with sand between the layers. Yet by the nineteenth century, by which time most of the Plains tribes had witnessed the reality of firearms penetration, such armor had largely been discarded and the warrior would ride into battle in his soft clothing.

WARRIOR SOCIETY

Although the Plains Indian tribes never replicated the hierarchical intricacies of European armies, this is not to say that they did not have their own rank systems. Each tribe would be headed by its chiefs, of which historian Richard Hook notes two fundamental divisions:

"While the structure of each tribe's authorities was complex, the most general distinction between leaders was that between the war chief and civil chief. The civil chiefs were generally senior, older men, concerned with the day to day life of the tribe; while war chiefs—the officers of the warrior societies—were vigorously involved in martial affairs."

– *Hook* (1985)

Spear
A short Plains Indian spear, designed more as a thrusting rather than a throwing weapon. The spear here is decorated with feathers and sections of rabbit fur.

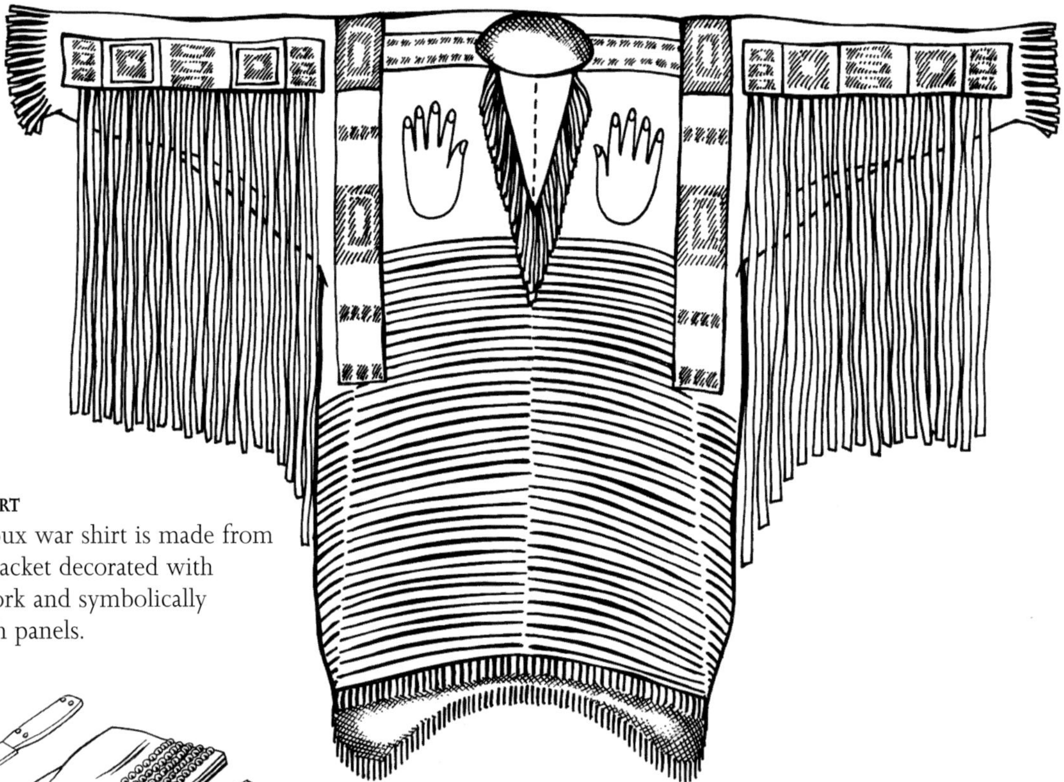

Sioux War Shirt
This classic Sioux war shirt is made from a tanned skin jacket decorated with tassels, beadwork and symbolically decorated cloth panels.

Dagger and Sheath
Steel daggers were acquired from the settlers, and came to replace earlier flint or copper blades by the end of the 18th century.

Sioux War Club
This Sioux war club features a lethal spike protruding out from the ball head. The spikes could be wood, bone or metal.

▲ **Sioux warriors on horseback in war bonnets, and carrying lances and shields. In combat, lances were sometimes thrown or used as hand-held weapons in a manner similar to European cavalry.**

Hook goes on to point out that the "idea of the Plains Indian chiefs as autocrats is mythical," demonstrating that they held their positions largely on a consensual basis, noting that "a poor chief would soon lose his position, while the band of a popular leader would prosper, and expand" (Hook, 1985). The meritocratic nature of Plains Indian leadership is important, for it goes some way to explaining the efficacy of Plains Indian resistance to the settlers. Furthermore, good warriors were highly respected throughout Plains Indian society, having influence in the tribe's council—a group of chiefs and elders who made major tribal decisions—as well as inspiring up-and-coming young men with the virtues of being a warrior.

Tribes also divided themselves into distinct warrior societies, these serving as both social and military clubs with their own rites, rituals, clothing and

▲ **A group of Plains Indians perform a war dance in full war outfit, brandishing flintlock muskets, stone-headed war clubs, spears and tomahawks. War dances could be performed both before and after combat.**

customs, and which served to give them status amongst the mass population of the tribe. Some tribes, such as the Blackfoot, Kiowa, Mandan and Arapaho, had a further complicated system for grading warriors within the society. The system for progressing up the ranks was a mixture of purchase, seniority and experience. Those at the bottom of the ladder—boys just coming to fighting age—bought their way into the lowest grade of warriors by offering gifts to those above. If their gifts were accepted, there was a ritual initiation and feast and the boys entered the warrior society, while those who had sold them membership attempted to buy themselves into the next grade. Unlike the British system of purchase, however, warriors had to demonstrate skill and courage in battle before they were allowed to step up in grade, the ultimate objective being to reach the top warrior grade in the tribe before retiring.

Not all of the Plains Indian tribes followed such systems, however. The Crow, Sioux, Cheyenne, Assiniboine, Pawnee and Arikara were all "non-graded" societies (see Hook, 1985, for a full discussion of the workings of Plains Indian warrior societies). Here there was a nominal equality between the warriors, although much like a star international soccer player, a well-experienced and highly regarded

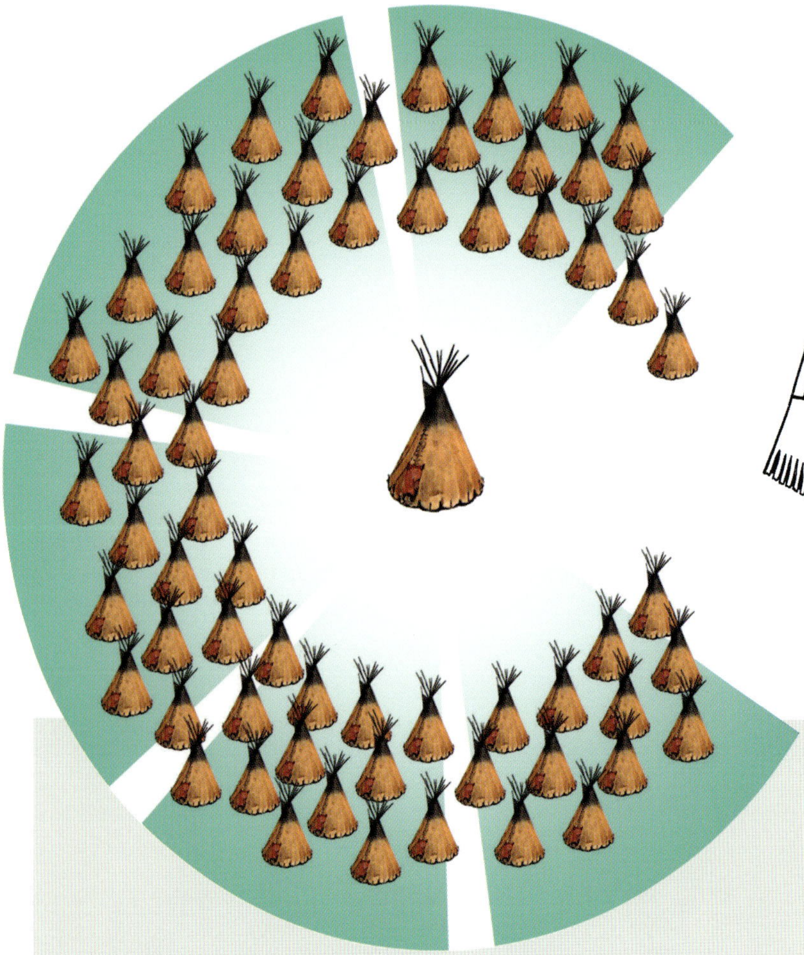

Camp Circle
A large Plains Indian village typically radiated out around the chief's tent in a circular pattern (depending on the terrain), divided by war bands. This configuration provided good all-round security.

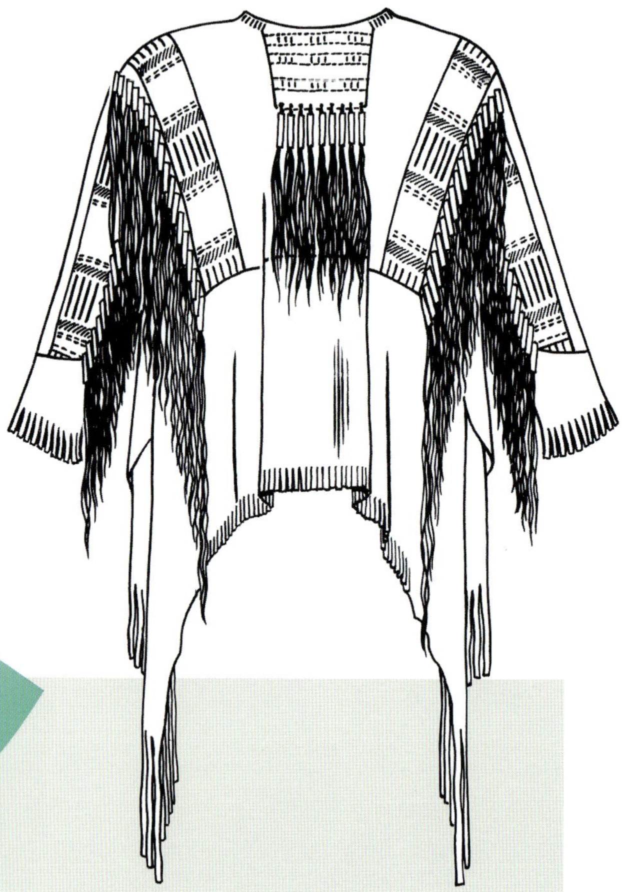

Lakota War Shirt
This Lakota war shirt features decoration of human or horse hair, and colored, beaded panels draped from over the shoulders.

▲ **An impressive photograph of a Sioux family in full dress. By the time this photograph was taken, in the late nineteenth century, the Sioux had largely been confined to reservations after defeat in the Indian Wars.**

warrior would be the object of other societies' envy, and they would attempt to attract him away from his existing society with gifts.

The societies were fiercely competitive, even abducting wives from their rivals, and demonstrating absurd bravery on the field of battle in attempt to raise the fame and notoriety of their own group. Hook notes, however, that being a highly regarded warrior was a double-edged sword: it conferred status and respect, but there were also obligations to keep showing near-reckless courage on the battlefield, often resulting in being injured or killed by enemy action.

Women

A little-studied aspect of Plains Indian society, at least in terms of its warrior culture, is the role of women. Some of the existing studies note that there is evidence of women joining Sioux war parties or raids, although the visual depictions tend to show women acting as baggage carriers for the fighting men.

Yet not all Indian women simply went along in a supporting role. Several Plains Indian women became respected horse raiders, such as the Crow Indian Woman Chief and Running Eagle of the Piegan tribe. The fact was that Plains Indian women were just as capable on horseback as any man, and the choice to be a female warrior was seen as unusual rather than an aberration. Furthermore, in bitter inter-tribal wars, and in the conflicts against the settlers, women and children were just as much targets as combatants. This became painfully apparent during the second half of

◀ Chief Bigfoot was a Lakota Sioux chief, and was one of the Sioux warriors most feared by the settlers. A diplomat as well as a soldier, he was finally caught and killed in the infamous Wounded Knee massacre (1890).

the nineteenth century, when Federal troops began what virtually amounted to a policy of extermination against certain noncompliant tribes.

A particularly notorious example is the "Wounded Knee Massacre," which occurred on December 29, 1890. The context of the massacre was the rise of the Ghost Dance religion amongst the starving and dispossessed Lakota Indians in South Dakota. One of the tenets of the new religion was the disappearance of the settlers, so naturally the US government became nervous that the reservation Indians might revolt. A US clampdown resulted in sporadic violence and the arrest of some Lakota leaders. Many of the Ghost Dance adherents now saw resistance as futile, including the Miniconjou chief Big Foot, who

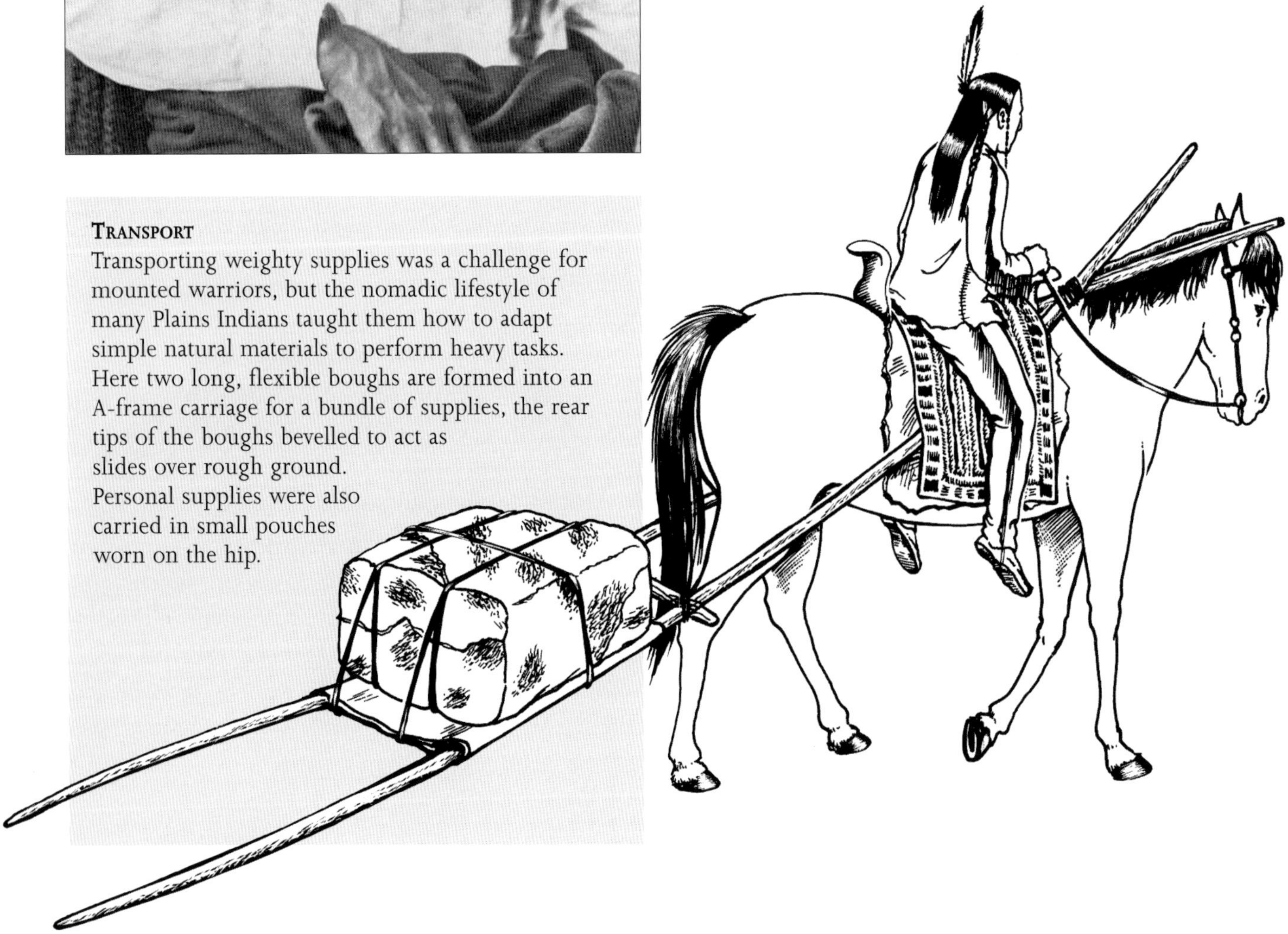

Transport
Transporting weighty supplies was a challenge for mounted warriors, but the nomadic lifestyle of many Plains Indians taught them how to adapt simple natural materials to perform heavy tasks. Here two long, flexible boughs are formed into an A-frame carriage for a bundle of supplies, the rear tips of the boughs bevelled to act as slides over rough ground. Personal supplies were also carried in small pouches worn on the hip.

▲ **A disturbing image of some of the Native American dead from the Wounded Knee Massacre in 1890. The Indians were killed by US Army artillery and rifle fire, and the dead included 44 women and 16 children.**

gathered 350 individuals around him and took them to the Pine Ridge Reservation in South Dakota, but they were forced by US troops to camp at the nearby Wounded Knee Creek. A large force of the US 7th Cavalry, 500 strong, promptly surrounded the camp, and even established artillery positions overlooking the native tipis.

On December 29, as the US troops attempted to disarm the Indians, a scuffle broke out and a rifle discharged. It was the cue for a massacre. The US troops opened up with their rifles and artillery and by the time the firing stopped up to 300 Indians were dead, a significant proportion of them women and children.

Such massacres were far from uncommon during the nineteenth century, and they proved that the idea of non-combatants was redundant. Therefore it is not unreasonable to understand how we hear of Indian women picking up rifles and fighting back—their own survival, and that of their children, was at stake.

CHAPTER 4

PLAINS BATTLES

The nineteenth-century geographer and ethnologist Henry Rowe Schoolcraft observed how closely tied Plains Indian tactics could be to wide

MAJOR ENGAGEMENTS: PLAINS WAR 1820–90

As this map illustrates, the entire High Plains area of the United States experienced major engagements between the settlers and the Native Americans. The cause of the Plains Wars was largely a matter of simple demographics—by 1870 there were about 40 million settlers in the United States, many of whom were pushing against the 300,000 Plains Indians in pursuit of agricultural land and buffalo hunting. Despite the Indians' generally superior warrior skills, they could not stop being swamped by sheer numbers.

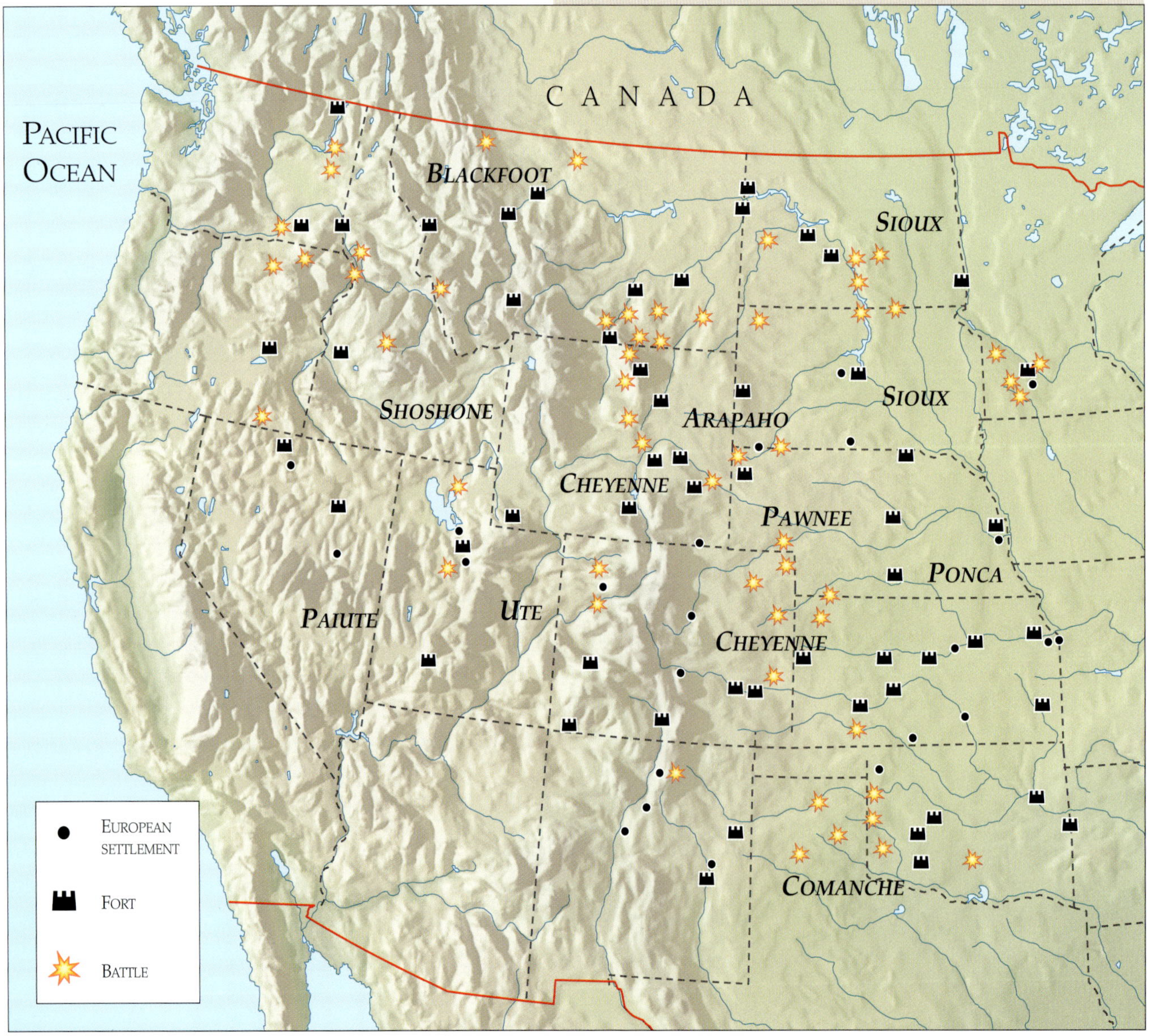

▲ **US cavalry and Plains Indians make an exchange of rifle fire from horseback. Although the settlers had many talented horsemen, the Indians took warrior horsemanship to near perfection.**

open spaces. Here he quotes one Lieutenant Pike, who makes observations on the contrasting tactics of the Chippewa and Sioux Indians:

"The Sioux attack with impetuosity; the others defend with every necessary precaution. But the superior number of the Sioux, would have enabled them to have annihilated the Chippeways long since, had it not been for the nature of their country, which entirely precludes the possibility of an attack on horseback. Also it gives them a decided advantage over an enemy, who, being half armed with arrows, the least twig of a bush turns the shaft of death out of its direction. Whereas, the whizzing bullet holds its course, nor spends its force short of its destined victim. Thus, we generally have found, that when engaged in a prairie, the Sioux came off victorious; but if in the woods, even, if not obliged to retreat, the carcasses of their slaughtered brethren shew how dearly they purchase the victory."

– *Schoolcraft* (1821)

Lieutenant Pike observes that familiarity with the terrain could be a constraint as well as an advantage. The Plains Sioux, according to Pike, lost the advantage of mounted warfare once they ventured off the prairie and into the woodland, the converse being true for the Chippewas. His view is not universally applicable across all the Sioux, since there were tribes that inhabited woodland and forest areas, and doubtless these were just as comfortable fighting in those environments as any other woodland tribe. Yet the plains and prairies undoubtedly required a unique set of skills to master in war, particularly in the fields of navigation and communication across such vast expanses of open ground.

In terms of navigation, an intimate knowledge of the local and regional terrain was of course built into the Plains Indian warriors from childhood. Settlers (those on friendly terms with the Indians, of course) would sometimes obtain charcoal sketched maps of surrounding territory, often finding these more accurate, or at least useful, than the maps produced by European cartographers.

Edwin Denig, a fur trader operating around Assiniboine territory in the 1850s, explained in one account that the chief had drawn him a map encompassing "a circumference of 1,500 miles" and that "so correct was the drawing that we had no difficulty in finding their camp the following winter in deep snow, one month's travel from this place" (Denig, 1930).

Of course, when maps based on local knowledge couldn't help, the Plains Indians relied upon ancient skills of navigation, such as reading the prevailing wind direction or navigating by the stars or the position of the sun. Migration patterns of animals, or the flight paths of birds, would often indicate the direction of water.

While travelling, particularly during a warlike expedition, the members of a war party also had to communicate with one another to convey intentions to those in distant sight or out of visual range. Such communication was particularly important between the scouts out front and the main war party following behind. Each war party would agree, or understand, a system of signalling. Ground messages were commonly used, these consisting of patterns of twigs and stones arranged on the ground. The warriors created V-shaped arrangements of materials, for instance, to indicate the direction of travel taken by the lead party, and different colored stones or pieces of charcoal would denote features, such as rivers, hills and camps.

Fetterman Defeat 1866

In 1866, in an act of bravado, Captain William J. Fetterman set off with 80 men, declaring that he could ride straight through Sioux territory with impunity. Following a party of Indian decoys, Fetterman went deep into Sioux territory before being ambushed at the later-named Ambush Hill and his party massacred to a man.

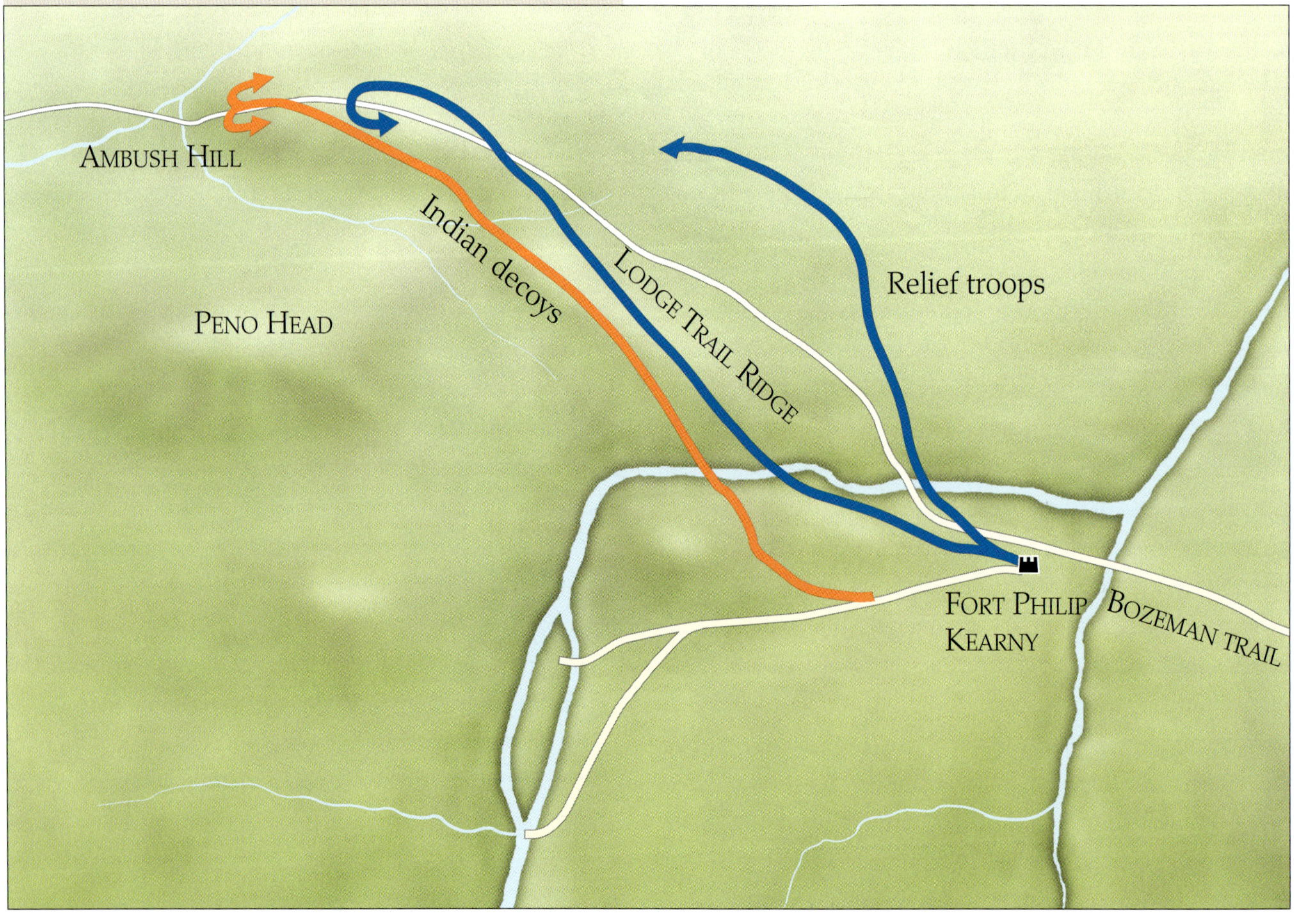

▲ **A party of Native American US Army Scouts track across the Plains. The US Army used Indian scouts owing to their superior field skills, particularly when it came to tracking.**

Apart from ground signals, the Plains Indians also used a variety of distance signals. Horsemen would ride in distinctive patterns, which would convey a message to their comrades observing them from afar. Signallers bounced sunlight off pieces of mirror or polished metal. Smoke signals were another option, these being used to both provide information and to coordinate separate forces. Washington Irving, writing about explorations amongst the Crow people, explains how smoke was used as a communication system:

"The travellers [the settlers] kept on their way due east, over a chain of hills. The recent rencontre showed them that they were now in a land of danger, subject to the wide roamings of a predacious tribe; nor in fact, had they gone many miles, before they beheld sights calculated to inspire anxiety and alarm. From the summits of some of the loftiest mountains, in different directions, columns of smoke began to rise. These they concluded to be signals made by the runners of the Crow chieftain, to summon the stragglers of his band, so as to pursue them with greater force. Signals of this kind, made by outrunners from one central point, will rouse a wide circuit of the mountains in a wonderfully short space of time; and bring the straggling hunters and warriors to the standard of their chieftain."

– *Irving (1836)*

Here the Crow Indians used smoke as a tool of centralized command, gathering different groups of warriors to the chief while also alerting them to a potential threat or target.

The Plains Indian skills at navigating, signalling, horsemanship and all aspects of warfare would be sorely tested during the nineteenth century, when they came up against their greatest foe—European settlers and the US military machine. Whether battling Texas Rangers, US cavalry or infantry, or just civilian settlers and traders, the Indians quickly realized that they had come up against a formidable opponent. While the settlers lacked many of the field skills on which the Plains Indians relied, they compensated with mental and physical toughness, skill with firearms (particularly in the case of civilian hunters) and their sheer numbers. When the two sides met in battle, therefore, the outcome was generally uncompromising and bloody.

Here we shall make a close study of two major Plains Indian battles—the battle of Adobe Walls in 1874, and the infamous battle of the Little Bighorn in 1876. Interestingly, these battles not only demonstrate traditional Plains Indian warrior tactics, but also the incorporation of some European military skills, illustrating that the Native Americans were open to learning from their opponents.

The Battle of Adobe Walls

The context for the battle of Adobe Walls was mounting tension between the Native Americans and the settler buffalo hunters. In the period following the Civil War, the situation for the Plains Tribes regarding the buffalo worsened considerably. Buffalo-hide clothing reached new levels of fashionability in the heavily populated Eastern territories, resulting in thousands of hunters flocking west armed with rifles. The result, as we have seen, was a massacre of the buffalo. At one point, a local store at the hunters' settlement of Adobe Walls, built around an abandoned fort in the Texas Panhandle, was receiving about 1,000 buffalo hides every day. The situation was made even more critical by the development of a new tanning process that made the buffalo's thin summer coat just as useful to the settlers as the long winter coat. In short, the settler hunters could kill all year round including during the breeding season. For the Comanche people, the time to act had come.

In mid-1874, the Comache chiefs Quanah Parker and Spotted Pony arranged a meeting with Kiowa, Arapaho and Cheyenne chiefs to discuss the situation. In an impassioned debate, the tribal chiefs agreed that

▼ A US Cavalry scouting party stop to reconnoiter an Indian village. While the soldier uses binoculars to scan the village, the Indian relies on naked eyesight—Indian scouts were known for their exceptional vision.

◀ **Quanah Parker was a famous Comanche leader, the son of a Comanche father and a European mother. An accomplished warrior, Parker died of natural causes in 1901, and his funeral was attended by 1,500 people.**

only violent resistance was going to stop the wholesale slaughter of the buffalo. It was decided that Adobe Walls had to fall.

On one level, the advantage seemed distinctly in the Indians' favor. The combined Indian war party that rode out towards Adobe Walls at dawn on June 27, 1874, numbered up to 700 warriors, whereas Adobe Walls contained merely 28 buffalo hunters and a handful of other civilian residents. Yet the hunters did have some advantages. First, they were well armed with Sharps and Remington buffalo guns, most in .44 and .50 calibers and all capable of dropping horse or rider at a considerable distance. Ammunition was plentiful—the local Rath & Co. store had more than 11,000 rounds available—and each hunter was also equipped with revolvers. Furthermore, the hunters had plenty of cover in their buildings. The hunters' habitations were constructed out of a mix of logs and sod, materials that in the right density can easily stop any bullet.

In classic style, the Indians attacked in full force, streaming down towards the settlement in full war paint with lances, guns and bows at the ready,

Comanche Territory 1860

The Comanche tribe's territory in the southern Plains meant that they were well-placed for raiding operations into Mexico and Texas. Although by the mid 1870s most Comanche were confined to reservations, their more skillful diplomacy meant they retained something of their traditional life.

◀ **At the battle of Adobe Walls in 1874, Comanche, Cheyenne, Kiowa and Arapaho Indians attacked a buffalo hunters' settlement in Texas. Although the battle saw the deaths of three settlers, the Indians sustained 15 deaths from accurate rifle fire, and finally broke off the attack.**

screaming their war cries. Two settlers who had been asleep in a wagon were shot and scalped, then the war party descended on the houses, circling around them as if they were so many buffalo.

After such a ferocious start, the battle steadily turned against the Indians. Horses and warriors began to drop from heavy-caliber rifle rounds, the buffalo hunters, fine marksmen all, selecting their targets and hitting them at several hundred meters. The Indians replied with volleys of fire, only to see them disappointingly absorbed by the hunters' buildings. Yet the battle of Adobe Walls was not just an exchange of rifle fire. Many Indians dismounted and moved in close among the buildings, emptying their revolvers and rifles through any gaps in the structure of the houses. The only way they could kill the hunters, however, was actually to enter the dwellings and fight at close quarters, but when they presented themselves at windows and doors they were shot down by the hunters' revolvers.

During the battle, the Indians applied some tactics that were derived from service in the US Army, as Douglas V. Meed in his book *Comanche 1800–74* relates:

"Uniquely, the warriors put some army tactics into practice. Warriors attacked, circled the buildings shooting, and then at a bugle call, fell back and regrouped. When the bugler blew the charge, they attacked again. Years later, Quanah would recount that the bugler was an army deserter who had joined the tribe. Wearing war paint and a feathered bonnet, he blew army bugle calls to direct the fighting."

– *Meed* (2003)

Although the bugler in this case was an army deserter, the fact that Quanah integrated the tactic into his battle plan is significant. It shows that the

Plains Indians learned some new techniques of battlefield coordination from the settler armies. Ironically, in this case the temporary withdrawals may have done more harm than good. By pulling back and gathering together, the Indians would have formed a good target for the hunters' long-range rifles, unless they managed to place themselves behind significant cover.

The battle of Adobe Walls ultimately deteriorated into one of attrition for the Native American attackers. Although three buffalo hunters were killed during the action, some two dozen Indians were dead and many more wounded, including Quanah Parker. In the end, the attack was broken off and the demoralized Indian force returned home. Worse still, the Adobe Walls action provoked the US government to launch a major campaign against the southern Plains tribes, which became known as the Red River War (1874–75). Over the course of a year of fighting, the Southern tribes were effectively ground

SCALPING

The origins of scalping are unknown, but it appears to have arisen among some (but not all) Native American tribes during the eighteenth century. For many Indian tribes, the scalp was regarded as holding a person's spirit, hence to lose a scalp was a shameful event, while to gain one produced a sense of victory—some celebrations following a successful scalping action could last for days, even weeks. Once collected, scalps were used in various ways according to tribal traditions. Often they were applied as decoration, hung from weapons, shields, clothing, horses, tipis and so on, visually demonstrating the power and victories of a particular warrior or society.

The actual techniques of scalping varied slightly. Some scalps consisted of a small portion of hair and skin cut around the crown of the head, whereas in other cases the incision ran in a circle from the forehead to the back of the head, leaving the victim virtually with an exposed upper skull. In most cases, a scalped individual would be dead, killed in earlier fighting, but scalping was also performed while the victims were still alive.

▲ An engraving imagines the last acts of the Fetterman Massacre, 1866, with Indian warriors cutting the scalps from both the dead and the living, and brandishing them as signs of victory.

▲ On November 29, 1864, a 700-strong party of the Colorado Territory Militia attacked a Cheyenne and Arapaho camp, killing 133 Indians, many of them women and children.

down into small scattered parties, desperately fighting for survival.

The Battle of the Little Bighorn

Adobe Walls shows how vulnerable the Plains Indians were when fighting an emplaced and sharpshooting enemy—in effect, they struggled to fight against an enemy who fought as they sometimes did. Against conventional forces, however, the battle could be tipped in their favor, especially if the opposing commanders made serious errors of judgment, such as in the case of the famous US cavalry commander Lieutenant Colonel George Armstrong Custer, in the battle known in US history as Little Bighorn.

The US wars to control the belligerent Sioux Indians had been rumbling on and off since the mid-1850s, and they would reignite in 1876. The source of contention this time was the Black Hills in Dakota, a region placed in the Great Sioux Reservation by the Fort Laramie Treaty of 1868. However, during the 1870s pressure built on the US government to buy back the Black Hills to aid railroad development and prospecting. Settlers exploring the Black Hills had frequently met violent and understandable xenophobia from the Lakota, who also took to raiding non-Indian settlements, and the US government was moved to deliver a simple choice to the Indians—hand over the Black Hills, or face military action. It came down to the latter.

In the spring of 1876, US forces under the command of General Philip Henry Sheridan set out in what they hoped would be a decisive action against the Lakota and their allies, the northern

Cheyenne. There were three columns deployed, the aim being to trap the opposing Indians in a pincer movement. A "Montana column" (450 men) under Colonel John Gibbon set out from Fort Ellis, Montana, while General Alfred H. Terry led a column of 925 men from Fort Abraham Lincoln. Terry's column included the 7th Cavalry under the command of the headstrong Custer. Another column of 1000 men, headed by General George Crook, left Fort Fetterman in May.

Terry and Gibbon were guided to their target—a major Lakota encampment on the Little Bighorn River—by the able guidance of allied Crow scouts. A plan was formed, which in essence involved Custer, with some 700 cavalry, attacking the camp from the south, driving the occupants against Gibbon's men descending from the north. Custer was given some leeway to modify the plan according to contingencies, which he duly did by altering the route of

US Seventh Cavalryman
Forged in civil war, the cavalryman returning to the western plains after 1865 was a better-equipped and better-led combatant than the Sioux had driven from the Bozeman Trail just a few years before. This sergeant carries a breech-loading carbine firing a 405-grain soft lead bullet with tremendous range and stopping power. His issue Colt revolver is reliable and rugged, if slow to load. Cartridges for both at this time could be carried in a hand-stitched cartridge belt or the more traditional cartridge box on the trooper's belt.

approach to the Lakota camp and, on June 25, splitting his forces into three main components: a scouting party of 115 men under Captain Frederick W. Benteen; three columns of troops commanded by Major Marcus Reno; and five columns of troops under his own command. While Reno moved directly at the southern end of the village, Custer took his force up the Little Bighorn, hoping to attack the Cheyenne part of the encampment from further north. Yet as Reno neared the Sioux tipis, a group of Lakota warriors sounded the alarm and the battle began.

The battle of the Little Bighorn has been well-documented from the US side but an excellent account of the battle from the Lakota point of view comes from Chief Red Horse, whose testimony was contained in the *10th Annual Report of the Bureau of American Ethnology* (1893). History notes that when Custer's men attacked the Indian camp, they had underestimated the numbers of Indians present, which may have been as great as 6,000 warriors, although about 3,000 is a more likely figure. Custer had around 800 men in his force. Yet notwithstanding the superiority in manpower, the shock of the US attack was still profound:

"The day was hot. In a short time the soldiers [Reno's battalion] charged the camp. The soldiers came on the trail made by the Sioux camp in moving, and crossed the Little Bighorn river above where the Sioux crossed, and attacked the lodges of

Battle of the Little Bighorn 1876

This map shows the (likely) lines followed by Custer and the other US cavalry soldiers during the Battle of the Little Bighorn. Custer seriously misjudged the strength and the positions of the Native American warriors he faced, and allowed himself to be outflanked and then surrounded. Driven into confined terrain, the final battle for his survival lasted for about an hour, but resulted in the complete destruction of his force. At least 280 US soldiers lost their lives in the action.

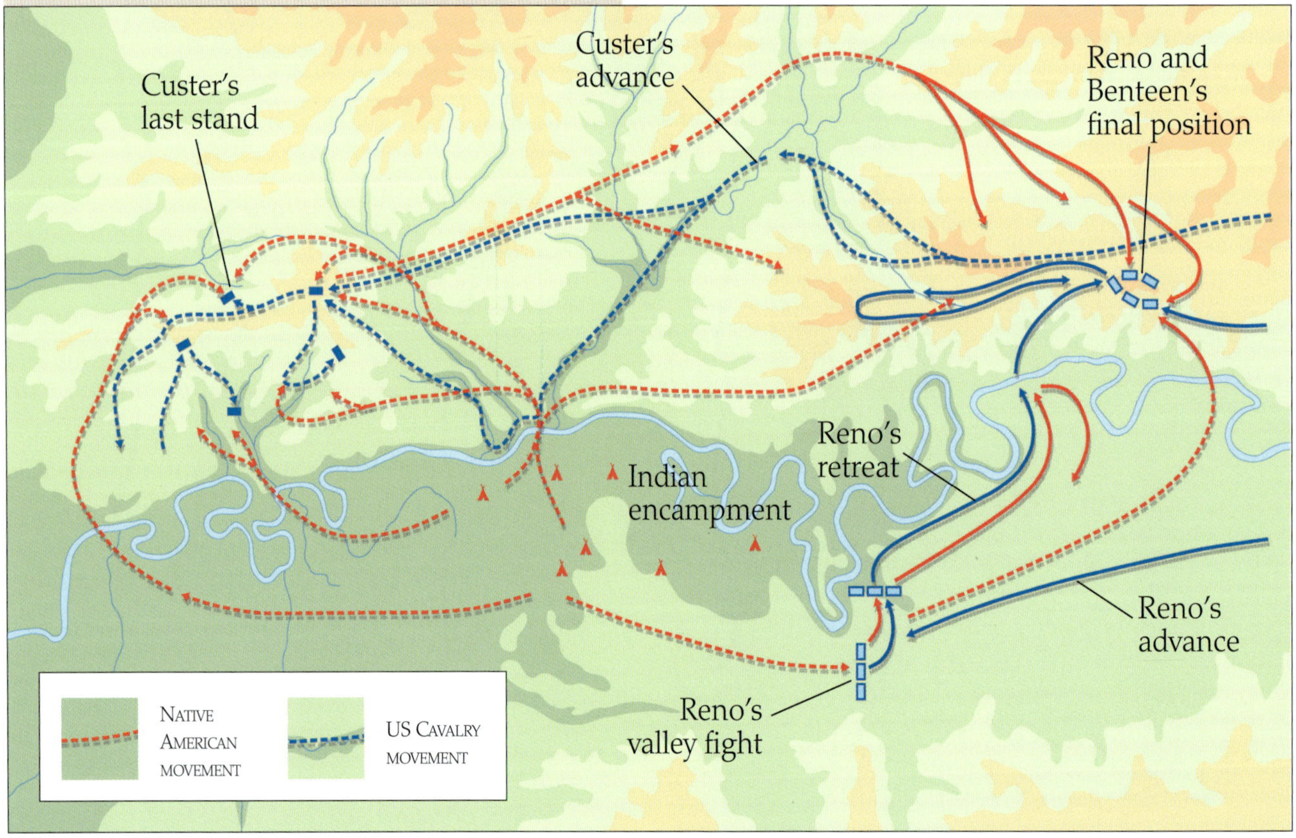

the Uncpapas, farthest up the river. The women and children ran down the Little Bighorn river a short distance into a ravine. The soldiers set fire to the lodges. All the Sioux now charged the soldiers and drove them in confusion across the Little Bighorn river, which was very rapid, and several soldiers were drowned in it. On a hill the soldiers stopped and the Sioux surrounded them. A Sioux man came and said that a different party of Soldiers had all the women and children prisoners. Like a whirlwind the word went around, and the Sioux all heard it and left the soldiers on the hill and went quickly to save the women and children."

– *Red Horse* (1893)

The defeat of Reno's attack was a critical early victory in the battle. Although initially thrown into confusion, the Indians responded well, counter-attacking with mounted troops who managed to outflank Reno's forces, which had been deployed in a defensive line. Once the Indians were confident that Reno was not going to come back at them (he had lost half his command in this engagement), they turned their attention to Custer's troops on the other side of the Little Bighorn. An assault across the river by Chief Gall of the Hunkapa band pushed Custer's men further northwest, driving them onto a high ridge, while other Cheyenne and Sioux bands joined in the attack from other directions. Red Horse's account of the battle gives a vivid portrayal of Custer's defense:

"... the Sioux charged the different soldiers [Red Horse uses the word "different" to denote Custer's men, as opposed to Reno's] below, and drive them in confusion; these soldiers became foolish, many throwing away their guns and raising their hands, saying, 'Sioux, pity us; take us prisoners.' The Sioux did not take a single soldier prisoner, but killed all of them; none were left alive for even a few minutes. These different soldiers discharged their guns but little. I took a gun and two belts off two dead soldiers; out of one belt two cartridges were gone, out of the other five.

The Sioux took the guns and cartridges

◀ **Sitting Bull was a famous Lakota Sioux holy man and warrior. He was a key figure in the defeat of Custer at the Little Bighorn, and a general focal point for Sioux resistance.**

off the dead soldiers and went to the hill on which the soldiers were, surrounded and fought them with the guns and cartridges of the dead soldiers. Had the soldiers not divided I think they would have killed many Sioux. The different soldiers [i.e. Custer's detachment] that the Sioux killed made five brave stands. Once the Sioux charged right in the midst of the different soldiers and scattered them all, fighting among the soldiers hand to hand.

One band of soldiers was in rear of the Sioux. When this band of soldiers charged, the Sioux fell back, and the Sioux and the soldiers stood facing each other. Then all the Sioux became brave and charged the soldiers. The Sioux went but a short distance before they separated and surrounded the soldiers. I could see the officers riding in front of the soldiers and hear them shooting. Now the Sioux had many killed. The soldiers killed 136 and wounded 160 Sioux. The Sioux killed all these different soldiers in the ravine."

– *Red Horse* (1893)

There is little sense of organized tactics on the part of the Indians here, purely opportunistic attacks and an aggressive determination to overwhelm the disorganized US command. Red Horse does hint at the fact that had Custer's command been unified in its defense then the battle might have turned out differently. At one point in the battle, some Indians even dressed in the uniforms of dead US soldiers, adding to the confusion of the US troops.

Custer's defeat was complete within about an hour. Of more than 200 men that Custer took above the Little Bighorn River, not one survived. Custer himself

Crow Scout
This Crow Indian Scout, a member of the US 7th Cavalry, wears a mixture of traditional Native American and regular US Army clothing (a military issue Army four-button jacket). The unorthodox dress indicates that this warrior probably dates to the early 1870s, for after 1876 Indian scouts were issued with full military dress. He is armed with the redoubtable Springfield 1873 carbine, a .45-caliber weapon that had a muzzle velocity of 1,350 feet per second (411 m/s) and a range of more than 3,280 feet (1,000m).

was found with two bullets in him, the one to his head probably added port-mortem. Following this action, the Indians sought to capitalize on their victory by pursuing Reno and Benteen, but the arrival of the rest of the US forces put them to flight.

The defeat at the Little Bighorn illustrates the fact that complacency among the enemy often featured in Plains Indian victories, indeed victories amongst any Indian peoples. Speedy horsemanship and the ability to travel fast on foot meant that the Indians could quickly take advantage of any tactical sloppiness, and such was the case at Little Bighorn.

▶ Major-General George Armstrong Custer performed poorly during his training as an officer cadet at West Point, and showed confused leadership skills during his final battle at the Little Bighorn. This photograph dates from the Civil War, where he distinguished himself as a impetuous cavalry commander.

▼ Indians with Winchesters chase panicked US troopers in the sketchbook of Sioux warrior Amos Bad Heart Buffalo, who served as a US Army Scout. His drawings represent an Oglala Sioux's record of the wars that ended his tribe's traditional way of living.

Glossary

adobe A clay used as a building material.
artillery Large-caliber guns.
autocrat A ruler with absolute power.
breech The back part of a rifle or gun barrel.
breechloader A gun in which ammunition is inserted in the breech instead of the muzzle.
brethren A fellow member of an organization; a male associate.
bugle A small brass instrument similar to a trumpet.
carbine A light automatic rifle.
cartridge A casing containing a charge and a bullet for small guns.
column A line of people moving in the same direction.
complacency A feeling of smug satisfaction with oneself.
escarpment A long, steep slope.
flint A hard gray rock used with steel to create an igniting spark.
flintlock A type of gun fired by a spark from a flint.
impetuosity Acting quickly and thoughtlessly.
Indian Removal Act A law signed by President Andrew Jackson in 1830 that authorized him to trade unsettled land west of the Mississippi for Indian lands within existing states, forcing tribes west.
massacre An indiscriminate slaughter of people.
meritocratic Power given based on ability and talent.
nomadic Wandering.
nominal A status existing in name only.
outflank Move around the side of an enemy.
projectile An object propelled through the air.
ravine A steeply sided deep, narrow gorge.
reconnoiter Make a military observation of a region.
redoubtable Formidable as an opponent.
scalping Cutting off the skin and hair on a portion of the crown of a person's head after killing them, as a trophy.
sod A piece of the surface of the ground with grass growing on it.
tipi A portable conical tent.

Further Reading

Cunfer, Geoff, and Bill Waiser, ed. *Bison and People on the North American Great Plains: A Deep Environmental History.* College Station, TX: Texas A&M University Press, 2016.

Hook, Jason, and Martin Pegler. *To Live & Die in the West: The American Indian Wars*. Abingdon, UK: Routledge, 2013.

Linde, Barbara M. *Native Americans in Early North America* (American History). New York: Lucent Press, 2017.

Lobo, Susan, Steve Talbot, and Traci L. Morris. *Native American Voices: A Reader.* Abingdon, UK: Routledge, 2016.

Sanford, William R. *Oglala Sioux Chief Crazy Horse* (Native American Chiefs and Warriors). New York: Enslow Publishers, 2013.

Wakim Dennis, Yvonne, Arlene B. Hirschfelder, and Shannon Rothenberger Flynn. *Native American Almanac: More Than 50,000 Years of the Cultures and Histories of Indigenous Peoples*. Canton, MI: Visible Ink Press, 2016.

Websites

IsumaTV
http://www.isuma.tv
The IsumaTV website is a multimedia archive containing work by indigenous individuals, with work speaking to their social, political, and cultural interests.

National Museum of the American Indian Collections Search
http://www.nmai.si.edu/searchcollections/home.aspx
The Smithsonian National Museum of the American Indian's online collection contains images of a vast array of Indian artifacts and art, both contemporary and historical. The collection is searchable by culture, region, artist, and object specifications, and contains detailed information on the objects' history and material qualities.

Native American History—Tribes, Battles, Chiefs & Culture
http://www.history.com/topics/native-american-history
The History Channel provides a collection of videos, articles, and images related to key figures and events in Native American history.

INDEX